I Can Read!

READING 3 ALONE

BUFFALO BILL
and the
PONY EXPRESS

story by Eleanor Coerr

pictures by Don Bolognese

HARPER

An Imprint of HarperCollinsPublishers

To Sarah and Cory
—E.C.

To Dom,
my old buddy who covers more ground
than a Pony Express rider
—D.B.

I Can Read Book® is a trademark of HarperCollins Publishers.

Buffalo Bill and the Pony Express Text copyright © 1995 by Eleanor Coerr. Illustrations copyright © 1995 by Don Bolognese. All rights reserved. Printed in the United States of America. No part of this book may be used or reproduced in any manner whatsoever without written permission except in the case of brief quotations embodied in critical articles and reviews. For information address HarperCollins Children's Books, a division of HarperCollins Publishers, 195 Broadway, New York, NY 10007.
www.icanread.com

Library of Congress Control Number: 93-24261
ISBN 978-0-06-023372-3 (trade bdg.) — ISBN 978-0-06-023373-0 (lib. bdg.) — ISBN 978-0-06-444220-6 (pbk.)

16 17 18   PC/WOR   20 19

CONTENTS

CHAPTER
❧ 1 ❧
RIDERS WANTED!

It was spring 1860.

Bill saw a sign in the post office

at Fort Laramie.

The sign said:

WANTED:

RIDERS FOR THE PONY EXPRESS

Young, skinny fellows under 18.

Orphans welcome.

$25 dollars a week.

"That's the kind of job I want!"

said Bill.

Bill went in to see Mr. Majors.

Bill stood tall and said,

"I want to join the Pony Express."

Mr. Majors laughed.

"A big wind could blow you away!"

he said. "You are too young."

"Gee whiz!" said Bill.

"I'm sixteen!"

"Don't try to fool me!"

said Mr. Majors.

"If you are sixteen,

then I'm a lizard."

"I guess I'm closer to fifteen,"
said Bill.

"Can you ride? Follow trails?
Swim? Shoot?" asked Mr. Majors.

"Yes, sir," said Bill.

"I roped cattle when I was nine,
and I can ride like the wind."

"It will be no picnic,"
said Mr. Majors.

"You must ride seventy or more miles
each day.

There may be trouble, too."

"I'm not afraid," Bill said.

"I like your spunk, son,"
said Mr. Majors,
"but you must promise not to lie,
not to swear, and not to fight.

And you must deliver the mail
on time, no matter what."

"I promise," said Bill.

Mr. Majors showed Bill a map.
"There's St. Joseph,
and there's Sacramento, California.
Eighty riders and four hundred ponies
carry the mail between these cities,"
said Mr. Majors.

"That's a long way!" said Bill.

"Yup," said Mr. Majors.

"It's about two thousand miles.
The riders travel all day and night
to carry the mail in ten days.
They are twice as fast
as stagecoaches."

ST.JOSEPH

Mr. Majors marked Red Buttes.

"That is your home station," he said.

"Your job is to take the mail from

Red Buttes to Three Crossings."

"More than seventy-five miles

on one pony?" asked Bill.

"Of course not!" said Mr. Majors.

"Along the way there are stations

with food, shelter, and fresh ponies.

After two days' rest,

you ride back with more letters."

Bill put on a red flannel shirt,

a red neckerchief, blue trousers,

riding boots, and a ten-dollar hat

to keep off the rain.

A shiny horn hung from his shoulder.

He was a real Pony Express rider now!

"Take these two pistols,

and a knife," said Mr. Majors.

"Just in case."

CHAPTER
⮞ 2 ⮜
THE CHASE

It was suppertime at Red Buttes.

The men swapped stories,

and Bill listened to every word.

"Remember when a herd of buffalo

trampled a rider and a pony?"

said Ben.

"Oh yeah," Shorty said.

"And remember when Paiute Indians

attacked a station

and stole the ponies?" said Ben.

"That's enough!" said Mr. Willis,

the station boss.

"Let's not scare young Bill."

At midnight,

Bill got ready for his ride.

His pony Bluetail was ready, too.

Suddenly a horn sounded.

Ta-tooooo! Ta-tooooo!

"Here comes the Pony Express!"
cried Ben.

A pony galloped in,
and the rider slid off.
Bill pulled the mailbags
off the tired pony
and put them on Bluetail.

"Giddyap!" yelled Bill.

Bluetail ran like the wind.

All of a sudden

Bill heard hoofbeats behind him.

The Paiute Indians!

Bill knew they wanted his pony.

"Faster! Faster!" he yelled.

Bang! Bang!

Bullets whizzed past Bill's head.

"Giddyap!" he shouted.

Bluetail ran as fast as he could,

and slowly the Indians fell back.

Bill was very glad

to see the lights of Three Crossings.

He blew on his horn.

Ta-tooooo! Ta-tooooo!

The stationmaster ran out.

"You must go on

to the next station!" he cried.

"The rider is sick."

"Oh no!" said Bill.

He was very tired,

but he changed ponies

and was off again.

Many hours later,

Bill returned home to Red Buttes.

He had ridden

long and hard,

and the mail was on time.

Everyone wanted to hear his story,

but Bill was so worn out,

he fell asleep at the table.

On payday, he sent money home.

He wrote:

Dear Ma,

The rides are easy

and the food is good.

Don't worry,

nothing much happens here.

I miss you.

Love, Billy

CHAPTER
≋ 3 ≋
WOLVES!

One night Bill was riding back

to Red Buttes.

A storm brewed.

Lightning crackled

and thunder rumbled.

Bill sang to calm his pony.

Just then rain began to pour.

Bill was soaked,

and the trail was slippery.

The pony had to slow down.

Then Bill heard

A-ooooo! Oo-woooo!

Wolves!

There were at least eight of them,

and they gathered around Bill.

Bill could see their eyes

gleaming in the dark

as they came closer and closer.

They bit the pony's legs and neck.

The pony reared up on its hind legs.

"I must not fall off,"

Bill said to himself.

"They would get me for sure,

and then they would get

my pony, too."

Bill fired his gun at the wolves.

They backed away.

Then Bill ran out of bullets, and

the wolves came toward them again.

Suddenly Bill remembered his horn.

Ta-tooooo! Ta-tooooo!

He blew louder and louder.

The wolves were so surprised,

they ran away.

Bill kept on blowing
until he saw the lights
of his home station.
"I'm sorry the mail is late,"
said Bill.

"I ran into some wolves."

"It's all right, kid,"

Mr. Willis said.

"The next rider will make it up.

Go get some rest."

The next day,

Bill wrote to his mother.

Dear Ma,

We had a bit of rain last night.

I was glad to have

the ten-dollar hat.

It kept my head warm and dry.

Love, Billy

CHAPTER
⇥ 4 ⇤
THE SHOOT-OUT

Bill was one of the best riders

on the Pony Express.

Everyone along the trail knew him—

even Chief Rain-in-the-Face.

Bill had gone to school

in Fort Laramie

with the Chief's sons.

They had taught him sign language

and the ways of the Sioux.

One day, Mr. Willis said,

"Bill, I want you to carry

a lot of money to Three Crossings.

Robbers are on that trail.

But I know you can handle them."

Bill was excited.

He liked danger.

Everybody talked about the money.

Terrible Tod heard about it, too.

"I will get that money," he said

to his gang of outlaws.

Bill knew he had to have a plan

to fool the thieves.

He went for a long ride

to think of a plan.

He met his friend

Chief Rain-in-the-Face.

The Chief was angry.

"Do you know what Terrible Tod

and his robbers are doing?"

he asked.

"They paint their faces like Indians

to rob and kill,

and we get the blame."

Chief Rain-in-the-Face

gave Bill an idea.

The next morning Bill got ready.

The Sheriff and his men came to help.

"We'll go along with you,"

said the Sheriff.

"Seven guns are better than one."

"That is not enough," Bill said.

"Terrible Tod has twenty in his gang.

But I have a plan."

Bill took off his Pony Express outfit

and stuffed it with straw.

"What are you doing?"

asked the Sheriff.

"You will see," said Bill.

He fastened a hollowed-out pumpkin

onto the straw man

and placed a hat

on top of the pumpkin.

The straw man looked like Bill!

All the men laughed.

"Pumpkinhead Billy!" they shouted.

They watched Bill put newspapers

into four mailbags.

Then he slapped Bluetail and yelled,

"Giddyap!"

Bluetail was off to Three Crossings!

Bill and the Sheriff and his men

followed the pony.

When Terrible Tod and his gang

saw the straw man,

they jumped out of their hiding place

and began to shoot.

They grabbed the mailbags.

Then the Sheriff and his men
surprised Terrible Tod.
There was a big shoot-out,
and Terrible Tod was caught.

Bill was safe.

He rode on to Three Crossings
with the money.

When he returned to Red Buttes,
there was a big party for him.

"Hurrah for Bill Cody!"

shouted Mr. Willis.

"I'm proud of you, kid," said Ben.

"Another story to tell your ma,"

said Shorty.

But Bill wrote:

Dear Ma,

Sometimes it isn't so quiet

on the trail.

I'll be home soon.

Love, Bill

AUTHOR'S NOTE

WILLIAM FREDERICK CODY was born on February 26, 1846. He joined the Pony Express in 1860. He was one of the riders who raced between St. Joseph, Missouri, and Sacramento, California, where a steamship carried the mail on to San Fransisco.

Many stories about Bill Cody and the Pony Express have become legends. It is difficult to separate truth from fiction since Bill himself loved to tell a tall tale. The incidents with robbers, the Sioux, and the Paiute Indians, however, really happened. Bill respected the Indian tribes, and he knew a lot about them because his father had traded with them.

The completion of the telegraph lines across the United States ended the Pony Express after only eighteen months. Bill and the other riders received medals for their part in carrying the mail.

Later Bill worked for the company that built the transcontinental railroad. He risked his life many times to supply buffalo meat for the workers. That is why he was called "Buffalo Bill."

Buffalo Bill died in 1917. A statue of him riding a pony stands near the Buffalo Bill Museum in Cody, Wyoming.